Darcy Daisy
and the Firefly Festival

Learning about Bipolar Disorder and Community

Lisa M. Lewandowski, Ph.D. and Shannon M.B. Trost, B.S.
Illustrated by Kimberly Shaw-Peterson

First Page Publications
Livonia, Michigan

Text © 2005 by
Lisa M. Lewandowski, Ph.D.,
Shannon M.B. Trost, B.S.
Illustrations © 2005 by
Kimberly Shaw-Peterson

Library of Congress Control Number:
  2005922695

Darcy Daisy and the Firefly Festival: Learning
about BiPolar Disorder and Community
/Lisa M. Lewandowski, Ph.D., Shannon M.B.
Trost, B.S.
  ISBN # 1-928623-52-2

Summary: Darcy Daisy is upset by rumors about
Ms. Zinnia's bipolar disorder. She shares her con-
cerns with her mother and gets answers to her
questions. Darcy gains a better understanding of
mental illness and realizes the importance of community support and acceptance.

First Page Publications
12103 Merriman Road
Livonia, MI 48150

Contact us:
www.dreamadifference.com
Email: shaytrost@att.net
Phone: (248)-672-6666

This book is dedicated to all those who are
open to seeing the strengths in our differences.

Thank you to the friends and family who never fail to offer their support, belief, and encouragement. This never would have happened without all of you. I am particularly grateful for Kenny and Syd's unconditional love and inspiration. Special thanks to Mom, Dad, Grandma Lewandowski and Michele for making the dream a reality, to Kathy for your thoughtful feedback and, of course, to Jim for his empathic ear.

~Lisa

Thank you to all my friends and family who believed in our dream and offered encouragement and assistance. Without you, this story would not have been possible. A special thank you to Karl for his love and support. Thanks to my mom, dad, and big G for their unwavering belief in me. An extra special thank you to Seton and Peyton for their enthusiasm, unconditional love, inspiration, and for their belief that their mom can do anything.

~Shannon

Thank you to the incredible people in my life who have encouraged me to follow my dreams and make them come true. Special thanks to Mom, Dad, and my amazing sisters for believing in me, the Peterson family for their loving support, and to Scott and Ella for inspiring me to create with my whole heart. Also, thanks to Rob, without whom I never would have been a part of this wonderful book.

~Kim

Introduction for parents, guardians, teachers, and health professionals

When someone is diagnosed with a mental illness, such as bipolar disorder, it impacts the individual, their family, and the community. Many families who have a member diagnosed with a mental illness keep their difficulties a secret. This secrecy can be an attempt to hide feelings, such as shame, or to avoid being stigmatized by those who fear or misunderstand the illness.

Unfortunately, mental illness is often misinterpreted and exaggerated by society at large. If children learn about mental illness, or the behavior of those diagnosed with mental illness, from indirect sources (rumors, television, or adult discussions partially overheard) then an already confusing topic can become a frightening one. It is essential that children are provided with accurate and direct information.

This book is designed as a springboard for health professionals, parents, guardians, and teachers to discuss some basic information about bipolar disorder; a medical condition with available treatment. It is intended to illustrate the importance of accepting individuals diagnosed with a mental illness. The book also highlights the strength of community cooperation; the importance of clarifying confusion and alleviating fear by collecting information from trusted others; and the harm that can result from stigma and gossip. These goals are accomplished through the experiences of young Darcy Daisy, a child who learns to accept people different from herself.

In the town of Merrygrove school has just let out. Darcy Daisy is talking about the Firefly Festival with friends Deena Daffodil and Lamont and Lakisha Lily.

"Can you believe Skipper the Spectacular is bringing his Breathtaking Bedazzling Butterflies this year?"

"I heard they actually perform the triple looper-de-boop move!"

"Don't get too excited," says Deena. "I heard that Ms. Zinnia may not be able to run the festival this year."

"What are you talking about?" Darcy asks. "Ms. Zinnia always runs the festival and they are always so much fun!"

Deena leans in and whispers, "I heard Ms. Zinnia has a really bad disease called buy-poles disorder and she is not doing a good job getting things ready for the festival. You have to stay far away from Ms. Zinnia too because you can catch buy-poles if you touch her."

"Sounds scary," says Lakisha. "What if they have to cancel the festival because Ms. Zinnia is too sick?"

Tears well up in Darcy's eyes at the thought of not having the Firefly Festival.

"I wouldn't believe everything you hear," says Lamont. "There's no such thing as a catchy disease called buy-poles. What would Ms. Zinnia do with a bunch of poles anyway? My mom always says that the only catchy thing around this town is gossip. Merrygrovers are always making things up without knowing the truth."

As Darcy passes by the café she hears the Bugleweed Club talking about Ms. Zinnia.

"I hear that Zelda Zinnia is seeing Dr. Cranium Geranium, the psychiatrist. I bet she is faking her problems just to get out of work."

"I think she's crazy. One day she cries at the drop of a petal and the next day she is so happy that she nearly jumps out of her stem!"

Carla Crabgrass snickers. "I saw her just the other day spending more pebbles and stones than she can afford. If she isn't more careful she will lose all of her money!"

At the corner Darcy sees Ms. Zinnia talking to Mayor Marjoram. She can barely understand what Ms. Zinnia is saying because she is talking so fast.

"Slow down, Ms. Zinnia," pleads the mayor. "I can't follow what you are saying. You are talking too fast!"

"I told you that I am in charge of the festival and things must be done my way!" Ms. Zinnia yells.

"Now Zelda, there is no need to get so upset. Let's sit down and talk about how you have been acting lately."

Darcy is worried and confused. She wants to hear more of what Ms. Zinnia and the mayor are saying, but she feels guilty for listening to their conversation.

When Darcy arrives home, she decides to tell her mother about her worries.

"Mom, does Ms. Zinnia have a bad disease?"

"Where did you hear that sweetie?" Mrs. Daisy asks, surprised.

"I overheard some things on the way home from school. I heard that Ms. Zinnia has buy-poles disease and then I saw her yelling at Mayor Marjoram."

"Well Darcy, I know that Ms. Zinnia has been diagnosed with an illness but it is called bipolar disorder, not buy-poles. It sounds like you heard some gossip. Sometimes when Merrygrovers are afraid of something they do not understand, they make up stories in order to explain it."

"Ms. Zinnia has told me a lot about her illness. At times she gets very, very sad. Not like you and me having a bad day, but so sad that she doesn't eat, has trouble sleeping, gets mad quickly, avoids people, and feels bad about herself. This is called depression.

"Other times Ms. Zinnia feels very, very excited. She gets so worked up that she talks too fast, often spends too much money, hardly sleeps, and becomes angry with anyone who tries to calm her down. This is called mania. The highs and lows she feels sometimes make it hard for her to get along with others."

"It was really scary to see Ms. Zinnia yell!"

"Now Darcy, take a deep breath. I know it was upsetting. I am glad you decided to talk to me about this. When you get scared or confused about anything, it is important to talk to someone you trust—like me, your dad, or your teacher."

"If Ms. Zinnia is sick, can't she go to a doctor?" asks Darcy.

"There is treatment that can help Ms. Zinnia. She can take medication, like you did when you had that sore throat. Medical doctors, or special doctors called psychiatrists, provide medicine. Also, Ms. Zinnia can talk to a therapist. A therapist is someone who helps you come up with ways to solve problems in your life."

Still puzzled, Darcy asks, "Mom, will I get sick from Ms. Zinnia?"

"Bipolar disorder is not something you can catch like a cold. It is not contagious, so you don't have to worry about that."

"I wish I could help Ms. Zinnia," says Darcy.

"Well, you can. You help her by being nice to her and accepting her. When Merrygrovers say bad things about her–things that are not true–it does not help Ms. Zinnia. Remember, she is just like everyone else in our community and deserves to be treated with respect and dignity. I know you would not like it if Merrygrovers were saying bad things about you."

Darcy agrees with her mom and feels much better.

In the next few days everyone sees that Ms. Zinnia is feeling better. Darcy and some of her friends help Ms. Zinnia get ready for the festival.

"Everything looks great Ms. Zinnia," says Darcy.

"Thank you. Getting help from Merrygrovers makes a big difference!"

Darcy grins. She feels good about helping someone in her community.

When the day finally arrives, the Firefly Festival is a great success!

"You know Darcy," says Deena, "I may not know much about Ms. Zinnia's illness, but I know she helped to make this one of the best festivals ever!"

Darcy nods. "Ms. Zinnia does get sick sometimes, but there is treatment for her. She will have some good days and some bad days, but at least there are things that we can do for her to help with the bad days."

"Yep. The worst thing is when people get scared and pass along the wrong information. That is bad for Ms. Zinnia and all of us," says Deena.

Darcy smiles. "Everyone is happier when we accept one another's differences."

The
End

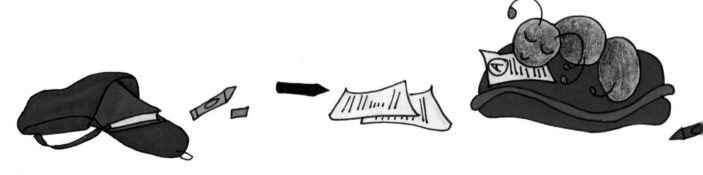

Additional Resources:

American Academy of Child and Adolescent Psychiatry—3615 Wisconsin Avenue NW, Washington, DC, 20016-3007; phone: 202-966-7300. www.aacap.org

American Psychiatric Association—1000 Wilson Blvd., Ste. 1825, Arlington, VA 22209-3901; phone: 1-888-35-PSYCH; www.psych.org

American Psychological Association—750 First Street NE, Washington, DC, 20002-4242; phone: 1-800-374-2721; www.apa.org

Depression and Bipolar Support Alliance (DBSA)—730 N. Franklin Street, Ste. 501, Chicago, IL, 60610-7224; phone: 1-800-826-3632; www.dbsalliance.org

National Alliance for the Mentally Ill (NAMI)—Colonial Place Three, 2107 Wilson Blvd., Ste. 300, Arlington, VA 22201-3042; information helpline number: 1-800-950-6264; www.nami.org

Authors' Bios

Lisa Lewandowski, Ph.D., earned both her Masters of Science and Doctorate in clinical psychology. She provides outpatient treatment to adults and is interested in family psychoeducation, women's issues in mental health, and trauma. In addition, Dr. Lewandowski works as a research associate for the University of Michigan, where she has been involved with studies exploring consumer-centered mental health services, coping and adaptation of mothers diagnosed with serious mental illness, and post-traumatic stress disorder. Dr. Lewandowski's most rewarding job, however, is parenting her young daughter, Sydney.

Shannon Marie Boyer Trost, B.S., earned her Bachelor of Science in psychology, with a concentration in social and behavioral psychology. Today she works at home as a free-lance editor, is active within her daughters' schools and extra-curricular activities, and uses her psychology background to aide in the everyday challenges of parenting.

Illustrator's Bio

Kimberly Shaw-Peterson is a self-taught artist and illustrator with a focus in painting. She currently spends most of her time illustrating from home, caring for her one year old daughter Ella, and working part-time as a floral designer. Kim has had the wonderful experience of teaching art to children through the Livonia Public Schools, being a creative partner in the set design for theater productions and painting murals for a number of schools and private homes. Kim plans to move forward in all her artistic endeavors by concentrating on illustration, and completing and exibiting new series of paintings.